CARSON CHOOSES FORGIVENESS

TONY & LAUREN DUNGY

Illustrations by GUY WOLEK

HARVEST **kids**

HARVEST HOUSE PUBLISHERS
Eugene, OR

To our children.
We pray you will find the courage
to honor God in everything you do.
Love, Mom and Dad

Cover design by Kyler Dougherty • Interior design by Left Coast Design

HARVEST KIDS is a trademark of The Hawkins Children's LLC.
Harvest House Publishers, Inc., is the exclusive licensee of the trademark HARVEST KIDS.

CARSON CHOOSES FORGIVENESS

Copyright © 2019 by Tony Dungy and Lauren Dungy
Published by Harvest House Publishers
Eugene, Oregon 97408
www.harvesthousepublishers.com

ISBN 978-0-7369-7322-9 (hardcover)
Library of Congress Cataloging-in-Publication Data

Names: Dungy, Tony, author. | Dungy, Lauren, author. | Wolek, Guy, illustrator.
Title: Carson chooses forgiveness | Tony and Lauren Dungy; illustrations by Guy Wolek.
Description: Eugene, Oregon: Harvest House Publishers, [2019] | Summary: Carson must decide
    whether or not to forgive star basketball player Daniel for making fun of him after their
    spat affects the whole team. | Identifiers: LCCN 2018054286 (print) | LCCN 2018057909 (ebook) | ISBN
    9780736973274 (ebook) | ISBN 9780736973229 (hardcover) | ISBN 9780736975889 (eBook)
Subjects: | CYAC: Sportsmanship—Fiction. | Teamwork (Sports)—Fiction. | Basketball—Fiction. | Christian life—Fiction.
Classification: LCC PZ7.D9187 (ebook) | LCC PZ7.D9187 Car 2019 (print) | DDC [E]—dc23
LC record available at https://lccn.loc.gov/2018054286

PRINTED IN CHINA

19   20   21   22   23   24   25   26   27 / IM / 10   9   8   7   6   5   4   3   2   1

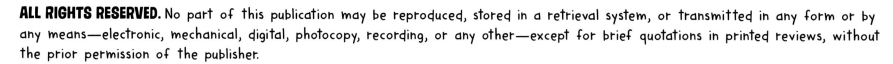

"Hey, Carson, hurry up or we'll be late for basketball practice!" Maria called impatiently.

"I'm coming, I'm coming,"
mumbled Carson, but his feet
dragged as he headed
toward the gym.

Carson wasn't looking forward to
basketball as much as he used to.

He didn't mind that he wasn't a starter. In fact, Carson was pretty good—but he wasn't the star of the Trentwood Elementary team. The star of the team was Daniel.

Daniel was the best
at everything—running,
shooting, dribbling—
and he knew it.

In the gym, Daniel was dribbling circles around a frustrated-looking Keiko.

Daniel spun and shot it over her head and through the net.

"Wow, did you see that?" he shouted.

"I can't miss!"

"Nice shot!"
said Coach Tony,
grinning. "Now let's work
on some drills before you start signing autographs."

Coach Lauren began assigning partners for the drill.

"Over here!" called Carson for the third time as Daniel dribbled past.

Daniel ignored him and took the shot, sinking it.

Maria looked over from her passing drill with Jaden. "Why didn't you pass to Carson? We're all supposed to get a chance to shoot in practice!"

Daniel shrugged. "But I never miss! And Carson hasn't made a shot in forever."

Embarrassed, Carson looked down at his shoes.

A sharp whistle
made them all jump.
Coach Tony stood
behind Carson,
looking stern.

"Daniel, I heard what you said about Carson. That kind of attitude is not okay. We're supposed to encourage our teammates."

Daniel nodded.

"All right, then," Coach Lauren said. "Line up for layup drills!" Daniel dashed off to be first in line.

The next day before their game against Grantville Elementary, everyone was still unhappy with Daniel.

"How can I get better if I never get the chance to shoot?" complained Carson.

"If he doesn't want to be a part of a team, then let's show him what it's like," Austin said, and everyone nodded.

Austin won the tip-off, and Keiko charged down the court with the ball, closely followed by a Grantville player.

Across the court, Daniel waved his arms. Keiko looked the other direction to Vanessa.

"I'm open!" shouted Daniel, but Keiko tried passing the ball to Vanessa.

Keiko's pass was intercepted by the defending Grantville player.

"I could have made the shot!" demanded Daniel, but Keiko ignored him as she followed Jalen and Jason after the ball.

Again and again, Trentwood players chose to pass to guarded teammates or try wild shots rather than pass to Daniel.

"Good," thought Carson. "Now he'll know what it feels like." But as the other team's score climbed higher and higher, he felt less and less satisfied.

Several of the players shot looks at Daniel.

"Daniel?" asked Coach Lauren.

Daniel looked up, his face red. "I don't know! Why will no one pass to me?"

"You said you didn't need any help to win," said Keiko.

Coach Lauren held up a hand. "When you have a problem with a teammate, instead of trying to get back at them, be honest about how you're feeling and give them a chance to make it right."

"Or ask your coaches to help you work it out," added Coach Tony.

"Daniel," Coach Tony said gently, "do you see how your attitude hurt your team?"

Daniel nodded, looking down. "I'm sorry I wasn't a better teammate," he said with a small voice.

Coach Lauren looked around. "Anger will weaken the whole team, and it won't make anything better.

The only way to move on from your anger is to forgive each other."

Carson thought about how unhappy they'd all been.
Standing, he turned to Daniel.

"I forgive you. And I'm sorry. Being angry was just as bad for the team as showing off." He held out a hand to Daniel, who shook it.

"Carson's right.
We can all be better
teammates," said Maria,
and she high-fived Daniel.
The rest of the team nodded.

"That's more like it!" said Coach Tony. "Now let's see
what a united team can do with this second half!"

"Yeah!" shouted the players, and they started for the court.

"Hey Carson," Daniel said, "that jump shot looked pretty good. Wanna try it again? Get open and I'll get the ball to you!"

Carson grinned. "Sounds good!" The boys high-fived and ran to join their team.

TEAMDUNGY

JOIN THE TEAM

THE TEAM DUNGY PICTURE BOOKS FOR
YOUNG READERS TEACH CHARACTER-BUILDING
LESSONS THROUGH THE WORLD OF SPORTS.

LOOK FOR MORE TEAM DUNGY BOOKS!

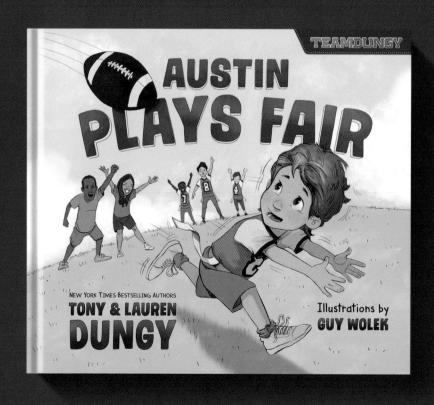

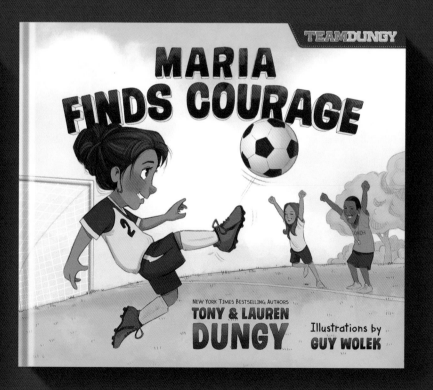

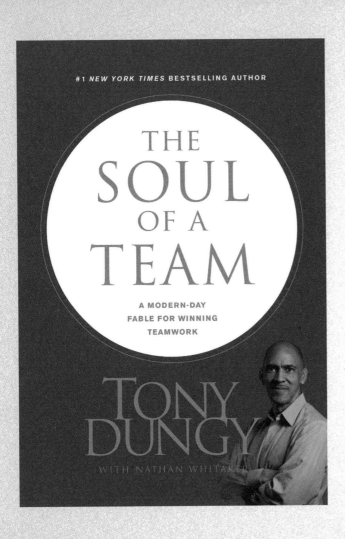